To all the children in the world who
believe in fairies and magic —K. H.

To Hilary, who shakes the fairy dust —S. W.

LITTLE SIMON

An imprint of Simon & Schuster Children's Publishing Division
1230 Avenue of the Americas, New York, New York 10020
First Little Simon hardcover edition January 2019
Text copyright © 2014 by Katherine Holabird
Illustrations copyright © 2014 by Sarah Warburton
Originally published in Great Britain in 2014 by Hodder Children's Books
All rights reserved, including the right of reproduction in whole or in part in any form.
LITTLE SIMON is a registered trademark of Simon & Schuster, Inc.,
and associated colophon is a trademark of Simon & Schuster, Inc.
For information about special discounts for bulk purchases, please contact
Simon & Schuster Special Sales at 1-856-506-1949 for business@simonandschuster.com.
Manufactured in China 1018 SCP
2 4 6 8 10 9 7 5 3 1
Cataloging-in-Publication Data is available from the Library of Congress.
ISBN 978-1-5344-2915-4
ISBN 978-1-5344-2916-1 (eBook)

Twinkle

Katharine Holabird and Sarah Warburton

LITTLE SIMON

New York London Sydney Toronto New Delhi

Twinkle's wings were
glowing with excitement!

"Tra-la-la-la-la!" she sang.
"I'm a little fairy
with sparkling wings.
When I get my magic wand,
I'll do amazing things!"

It was Twinkle's first day at
The Fairy School of Magic and Music,
and she couldn't wait to learn fancy
spells like all the big fairies.

Twinkle skipped in line with all the little fairies waiting for wands.

Her wish came true when she got a sparkling peachy pink one!

Shiny fairy notebooks and glittery pens appeared on all the desks.

Welcome to Fairy School

Buttercup
Izzybell   Pippa
Lulu   Tabitha
Petal   Twinkle

"...*tree!*"

Before she could blink, Twinkle found herself perched way
up in a pear tree with Pippa and Lulu waving below.

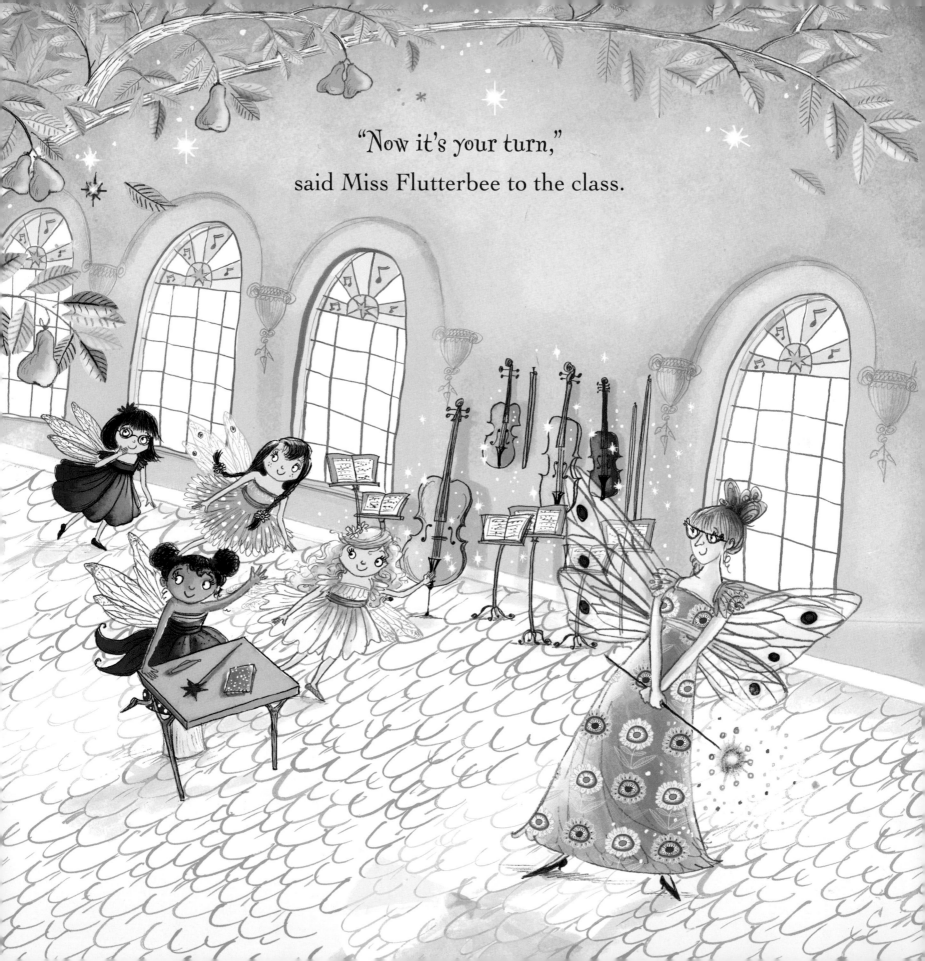

"Now it's your turn,"
said Miss Flutterbee to the class.

Pippa and Lulu sw**o**o**o**shed
their wands and . . . bingo!

They were both happily
dangling from a plum tree.

Twinkle tried s*wooshing* her wand,
but she got it all wrong, and instead of
sitting in a plum tree she landed
upside
down
in a prickly holly bush!

"Ouch!" cried Twinkle,
and Miss Flutterbee had to rescue her.

"Now remember to practice at home," said
Miss Flutterbee. "But **no** spells at night—
you don't want to start a ruckus."

That afternoon Twinkle and her friends did their homework together.

"This is fun!" said Pippa, turning a teapot into a tiara.

"I love doing spells," said Lulu, changing bananas into balloons.

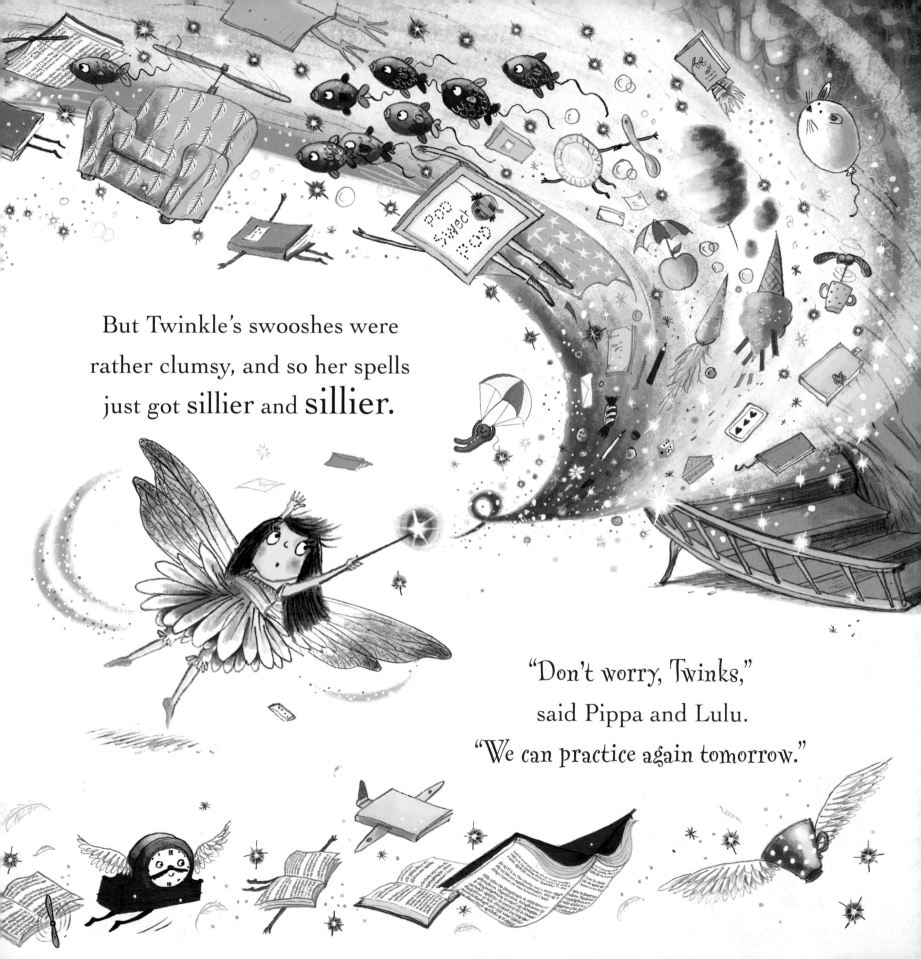

But Twinkle's swooshes were rather clumsy, and so her spells just got sillier and **sillier.**

"Don't worry, Twinks," said Pippa and Lulu. "We can practice again tomorrow."

That night Twinkle was in such a tizzy, she couldn't sleep a wink, and she forgot all about Miss Flutterbee's warning.

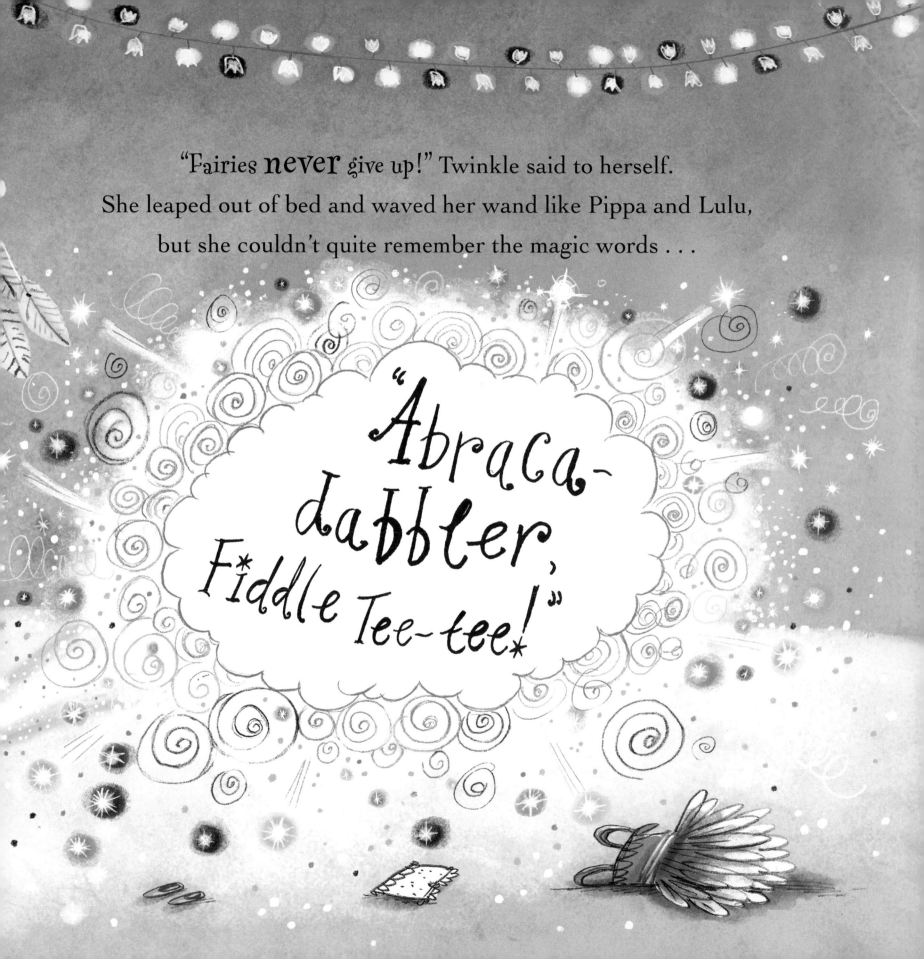

"Fairies **never** give up!" Twinkle said to herself.
She leaped out of bed and waved her wand like Pippa and Lulu,
but she couldn't quite remember the magic words . . .

"Abraca-dabbler, Fiddle Tee-tee!"

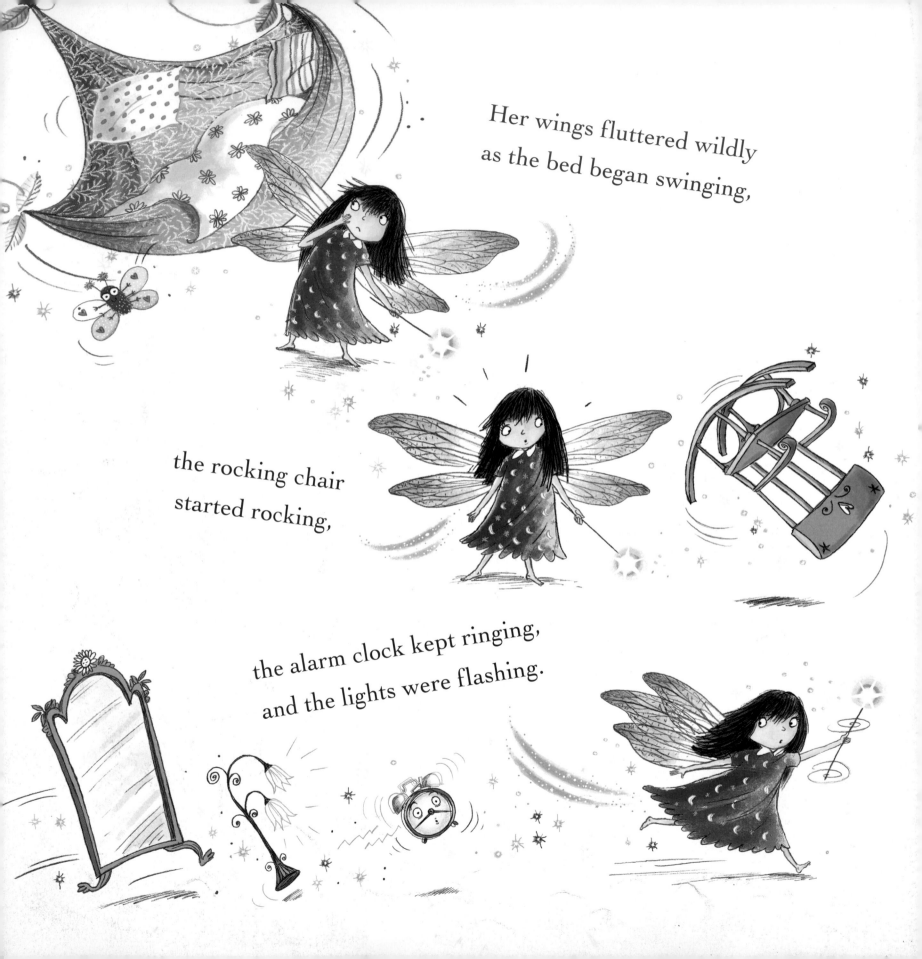

Her wings fluttered wildly
as the bed began swinging,

the rocking chair
started rocking,

the alarm clock kept ringing,
and the lights were flashing.

Twinkle's cozy little fairy pod was shaking
and swaying, banging and clanging.

"HELP!" shouted Twinkle as the rumpus continued.

One by one all the creatures in Sparkle Tree Forest woke up, and they were not very happy. . . . Bumblebees and ladybugs buzzed, grumpy gremlins and bullfrogs croaked, and groggy birds and bats fell out of the trees.

"Whoooooo'S making that racket?" screeched the owl.

"Stop the ruckus!" shouted the squirrel.

"**Fiddlesticks and Fairy cakes!**"
said Twinkle, waving her wand faster and faster, but the crashing and banging only got louder.

The next morning every creature in the forest was
howling and complaining outside Twinkle's door.

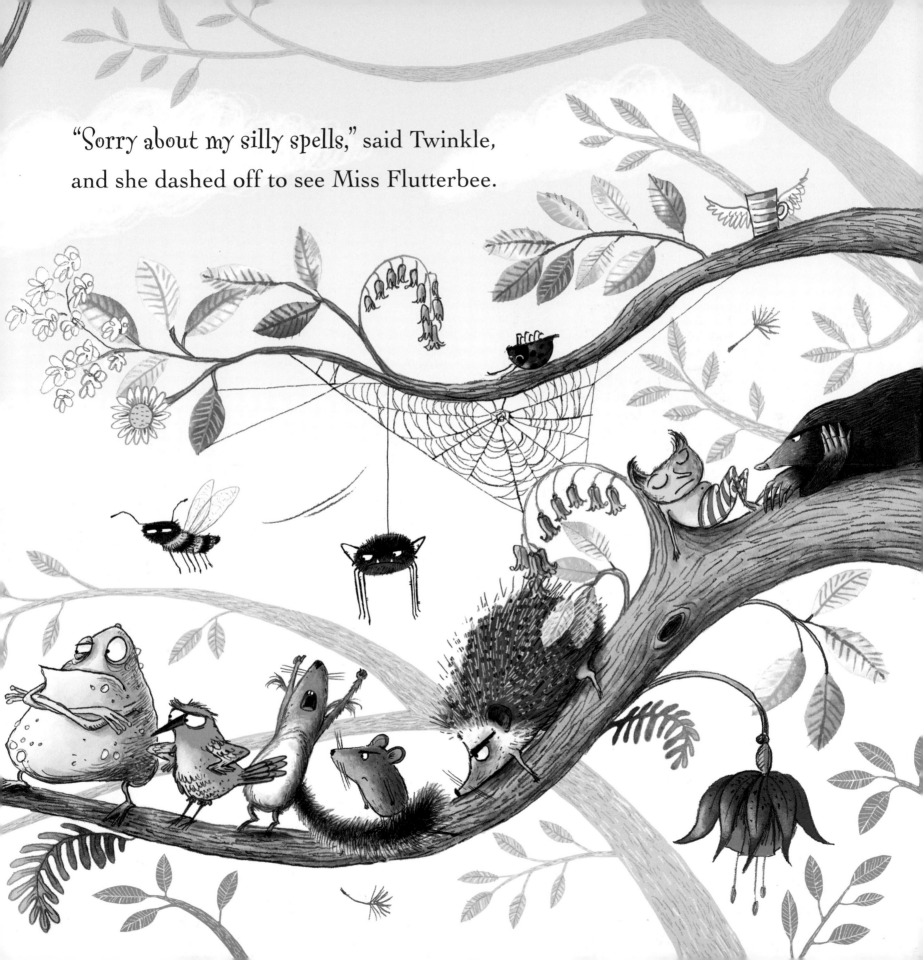

"Sorry about my silly spells," said Twinkle, and she dashed off to see Miss Flutterbee.

"Gracious gremlins!" said Miss Flutterbee in surprise when she saw the parade of insects and animals following Twinkle.

"I'm having a spot of trouble with my homework," said Twinkle. "I keep forgetting the magic words!"

"Since you love to sing, try **singing** your spells instead.
Maybe that will help you remember," suggested Miss Flutterbee kindly.

"Brilliant!" said Twinkle,
and her wings glowed
bright pink again.

After school that day Twinkle flew home singing the magic words.

"Abracadabra, skidddle-dee-dee, fix the mess that's up in my tree."

And when she arrived, Twinkle was overjoyed to
see everything was back in its place again.

As the sun set over Sparkle Tree Forest, Twinkle sprinkled fairy dust over the treetops and sang a lullaby to all the forest creatures just to make sure they all had a really good sleep.

"Good night, sleep tight, with sweet dreams in your head.

Tomorrow we'll have lots of fun, but now it's time for bed!"